Gavin & the Jingle Gulls

BY SALLY LLOYD

FOREWARD
BY GAVIN THE GULL

Many humans have a negative view of us gulls. We get bad press. Almost every day, you see something about how a seagull nicked a human's chips or ice cream.

Hopefully this story will show a better side of us, even though there is a fair amount of gobbling that goes on...

Did you know that we gulls can remember a human face? This matters for two reasons: one, it means that if you feed us, we will remember and seek you out again. Two, if you harm us, we will remember that too.

We know we shouldn't be eating chips, burgers, pizza, and ice cream, but it's only what you leave behind or eat in front of us.

We eat to live, not just for pleasure. Food is our survival.

This is the story of the Jingle Gulls, who form a band to help gulls who have fallen on hard times.

It is funny and heartwarming, and with a bit of luck, it will make you see us gulls in a better light.

Note by the Author

Gavin the Gull has long been the mascot for my photography business. He's a special gull, and much loved. I hope you will enjoy hearing about his adventures.

I wrote this book in memory of our mother Dilys Lloyd, who loved birds, biscuits and books.

Gavin & The Jingle Gulls

"The trouble with you lot," Gavin glared at his band, "is that all you think about is food!"

"So says the gull who, last night, came back with the biggest burger I have ever seen." Gobbler grunted into his wing.

"I heard that." Gavin narrowed his beady eyes. "If we are going to be ready to play at the Nelson's Good Eye Pub Christmas charity gig, you've all got to practice. Those instruments won't play themselves." Gavin blinked. "There will be plenty of free food, but if we aren't any good, we are more likely to have it thrown at us rather than to us."

"I don't mind." Dropper always dropped his anyway.

Gobbler sat up straight; he didn't like the thought of missing out on free food. "My guitar needs tuning, but I will play it every morning and every night until I master the tunes. What are they again?"

Gavin sighed. "You mean the playlist?"

Gobbler looked confused. "I mean, what tunes are we going to play?"

Screecher screeched with laughter. "Christmas tunes, of course!"

Gavin groaned. What hope did he have in getting this unruly lot to create a band worth listening to? They could knock out a sea shanty or two, but ask them to apply themselves to anything different, and they fell apart.

"We are going to have nightly practice sessions, and I expect all of your instruments to be in perfect working order. No excuses."

"Ooh er." Stasher rolled his eyes.

"What's that under your wing?" Gobbler could see something moving.

"Nuffing." Stasher shifted uncomfortably.

"It's a fish!" Screeched Screecher, "I just saw its tail flick."

"And no extra creatures or food will be allowed into practice sessions." Gavin's steely squawk left the gulls rigid. "No distractions. Do you all hear me?"

His motley crew of seagull musicians meekly nodded their heads.

"Now off you fly, and I'll see you Jingle Gulls back here on the roof tomorrow night at 7 p.m. sharp."

"He talks to us like he's a sergeant major or something," grumbled Stasher as he waddled out, trying to keep the flapping fish beneath his wing under control.

"Why do you keep a live fish under your wing?" Gobbler eyed it greedily.

"So it's fresh when I present it to Mindy. She's fussy about her fish."

Gobbler rolled his eyes. "High Maintenance Mindy."

At 6.45 p.m. the next night, Gavin paced the rooftop, looking out over the edge, hoping his band of Jingle Gulls wouldn't let him down.

Slowfly glided down gracefully five minutes later, swiftly followed by Gobbler and Stasher.

"Any sign of Dropper?" Gavin squawked at them.

"Ah," Gobbler looked uncomfortable. "He's gone off in a strop."

"Why?"

"Well..." Gobbler started to explain, but a furious flapping of wings made them look up to see Dropper hovering above.

"Tell him to give me back my kebab, and then, only then, will I come down to practice." Dropper screeched furiously.

Gavin glared at Gobbler. "What's this?"

"I er..."

Dropper swooped down, stamping his feet on the rooftop tiles. "I'll tell you what he did," he screeched, pointing a wing in Gobbler's direction. "I had been watching a clubber down the Prince of Wales Road with a juicy-looking kebab for at least half an hour, and the clubber started to talk to a girl and left his kebab on a window sill. I grabbed it quick but lost my footing and dropped it onto the pavement, and before you could even blink, Gobbler here swooped in and grabbed it. It's not fair!" He stamped his foot and waved his wings above his head. "I haven't eaten all day. You know I drop things, you've got no empathy!"

"Eh?" Gobbler looked confused. "What's that mean?"
"Exactly!" Squealed Dropper, his beak glowing with anger. "You are an ignorant gull."

Gavin sighed. "Give him back his kebab Gobbler, then we can get on with our practice."

But of course, Gobbler had already gobbled up the kebab. Not a morsel was left.

"I'll go and find you another one later. How was I to know you'd been after it for half an hour?" Gobbler sounded marginally regretful.

"Can we get on and practice?" Gavin's steely glare tried to steer them back to why they were here on the rooftop.

"I'm starving." Dropper whined, "How can I concentrate with an empty belly?"

"Don't be such a baby!" Stasher had had enough of this argument.

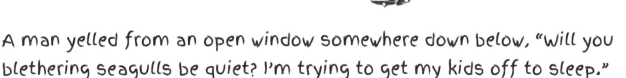

"I'm not a BABY!" Wailed Dropper.

A man yelled from an open window somewhere down below, "Will you blethering seagulls be quiet? I'm trying to get my kids off to sleep."

"Come on, we are all here now. Let's go down to the Seaweed Café, my missus will give me big trouble if I don't get back before sunrise. We've got nippers to teach how to fly tomorrow." Slowfly had his own problems. He knew that if his chicks took after him, they'd be as unlucky at grabbing food as Dropper.

The seagulls swooped off the rooftop in the direction of the Seaweed Cafe.

Every year, Gavin the Gull had the same problem with his Jingle Gulls. They weren't a bad bunch of gulls, but they did love to squabble over absolutely everything. Even the instruments they played.

Dropper didn't want to play a wind instrument in case he dropped it.

Screecher wanted to be the lead singer but had the most terrible voice.

Gobbler insisted on having an expensive electric guitar, and none of the other gulls were allowed to touch it.

Slowfly struggled with keeping tempo on the piano, on account of his slowness.

Stasher reluctantly agreed to play the xylophone but envied Gobbler's guitar.

There was no pleasing any of them.

At last, they all gathered around their instruments.

Gavin sighed a sigh of relief. "First on the playlist is White Christmas."

Gobbler sniggered.

"What's funny?"

Gobbler shot a sideways glance at Stasher. "Nuffing."

"Good. Now let's get on, shall we?" Gavin raised his wings like a conductor in front of his orchestra. He would do the singing; he'd given Screecher a tamborine and told him he could join in on the high notes. Gavin felt like he spent his whole life compromising.

Just as they'd finished the chorus, a rather regal looking gull wandered into the bar. The Jingle Gulls turned their heads simultaneously in her direction. Gobbler's beak fell open as if he'd seen food.

She turned her pristine white head towards them. "Play on, gulls, play on." Her voice was low, and Gavin noted that it was rather alluring. Suddenly, he felt nervous. He raised his wings to indicate that the Jingle Gulls should play.

Gobbler snapped his beak shut and twanged his guitar with verve.

"Now, Gobbler, we are not a rock band, we are a Christmas band. I am about to croon, not strut my stuff like Freddie Mercury." Gavin winked cheekily at the lady gull, who stared blankly at him. He coughed with embarrassment. Gobbler sniggered again.

"A one, a two, a one, two, three, four..."

A few bars in, and if you didn't know they were playing White Christmas, you would never know. Gavin's crooning could barely be heard above the random noises coming from the gull's instruments. It was as if they were all playing their own tune, and none of their tunes remotely resembled the song they were meant to be playing.

The lady gull raised her wings to her ears and grimaced. "STOP!"

Immediately, all the gulls started squabbling.

The lady gull raised a wing. "That's ENOUGH!"

The shock of her voice suddenly turning into a gruff bellow stopped the Jingle Gulls in their tracks. They all turned to stare at her.

"You." She pointed at Gavin, who immediately blushed. "Sing the song to me without anyone else making so much as a strum or a drum beat."

"That's what we need, drums," muttered Screecher under his wing to Gobbler, who stood frozen to the spot in awe of the lady gull's commanding tone.

Gavin began to sing. The other gulls had to admit that he did have a beautiful voice. They also noticed the dreamy look in his eyes as he sang to the lady gull.

The lady gull listened, her head to one side. Then, when he'd finished, she clapped her wings, slowly but with emphasis.

"Jolly good." Her voice returned to its previously silky tone. "At least one of you has talent. Now you with the guitar. Let's hear you play the song on your own."

Gobbler raised his guitar with aplomb, giving a little shake of his hips, then launched into a made-up riff before he actually started the song. He played every note with emphasis and flair worthy of a rock star."

Slowfly smirked. "Such a show-off."

Screecher clutched at his Tamborine. "At least he's got something to show off with. All I've got is this stupid thing."

"Now you, you with the wonky beak." The lady gull fixed her gaze on Slowfly.

Slowfly touched his beak with a wing. "I haven't got a wonky beak." He felt highly indignant at this accusation.

"Yes, you have," said Gobbler. "That's why you can't fly in a straight line. It's not your fault - it's aerodynamics. It's why you are slow."

"PLAY!" The lady gull had limited patience, just like Gavin.

Slowfly messed up the first few bars, but once he was in full flow, his natural slowness suited the song well. So well, in fact, that when he finished, they all clapped.

"See, it doesn't matter about your wonky beak." Smirked Gobbler.

"I haven't got a WONKY BEAK! Squealed Slowfly, and all the gulls laughed.

"Don't worry," said Dropper, "we've all got our quirks. Gobbler's got a big gob, that's why he's always gobbling up everyone else's grub."

Gobbler didn't want to look bad in front of the lady gull, so he kept quiet this time.

Stasher coughed. "Now me?" You could hear his nerves.

The lady gull looked around. "You and the one with the Tamborine. Bit of an odd combination, but do your best."

Screecher reluctantly wobbled over to stand by Stasher. He noticed that Stasher had something wriggling under one of his wings again, but he chose to ignore it.

Somehow, the thing wriggling under Stasher's wing didn't affect his playing of the xylophone, and he actually did a reasonable job. At least, the tune was vaguely recognisable. Screecher gave his Tamborine a little shake here and there to make it sound more Christmassy.

They finished, and the lady gull waggled her head at them. Neither of them knew quite how to take this, but at least it wasn't a screech of horror.

The lady gull eyed them all with interest.

The Jingle Gulls stood to attention as if being inspected, which, in truth, they were.

"Individually, that's not half a bad job. Collectively..." The lady gull sighed, "Well, let's just say, there's a significant amount of work to be done.

Gavin sighed, "We are only two weeks away from our Christmas Eve charity gig at the Nelson's Good Eye Pub. The truth is, I got carried away boasting to the landlord that I have this amazing band, the Jingle Gulls, who will blow everyone's socks off. Now I feel like an idiot. Anyway, may I be so bold as to ask you your name? I don't think we've met before."

The lady seagull blinked. "You don't recognise me?"

Gavin's thoughts spun through all the lady seagulls he'd chatted up over the years, but none were as classy as this one. He shook his head.

"I am..." She paused for effect. "Lady Serena Seagull of..."

Without meaning to, Slowfly finished her sentence, "The Seagull Songstresses. The biggest seagull band of all time!"

"Ensemble, actually."

Gavin's beak fell open; how could he not have twigged? He moved forward, his wings outstretched. "I am humbled to meet you, Lady Serena." He was practically on his skinny little knees in deference. "Please forgive me for being so ignorant. This is a great honour, a great great honour."

Gobbler thought he was going to throw up in his own beak. He tried to look cool. "Yeah, nice to meet you and all that. You must think we are a right band of plonkers."

Screecher groaned. "Yeah, this is embarrassing."

Completely dumbfounded by being in the presence of a celebrity, Stasher finally let go of what was under his wing. A warbling pigeon flew up to a rafter in the Seaweed Cafe and promptly plopped a poo straight on Gavin's head.

All the gulls, apart from Lady Serena, screeched with laughter as Gavin flapped his wings, trying to wipe the slippery poo out of his eyes.

"He really is Lord Muck now," sniggered gobbler. "Perfect for Lady Selena."

Luckily, neither Gavin nor Lady Serena heard this remark, but Screecher did, and he became hysterical with laughter. Bending double, he fought to catch his breath.

"Someone get me a tea towel!" Squawked Gavin.

Slowfly ambled towards the counter.

"And hurry up!" Gavin, humiliated, was in a right old flap. wretched Stasher, he'd beat him with his own xylophone mallet when Lady Serena had gone. well, as soon as he'd gotten this filth out of his eyes.

Lady Serena retreated to a corner. What a commotion! It amused her, but she did *feel* for poor Gavin. She found him rather handsome, if a little arrogant. She saw potential in the Jingle Gulls, but they badly needed tuition. She'd have a word with the manager of the Seagull Songstresses to see *if* she could help. It would be a shame if the Jingle Gulls missed their special Christmas Eve charity gig simply because they couldn't hold it together as a band. They were something quite unique, that was for sure.

Stasher sidled over to her. "I'm really sorry about this. I don't usually keep *live* food with me."

"That's a *lie!*" Screeched Screecher.

Gobbler overheard and butted in. "The truth is, he's never had the killer instinct. He keeps them for a while, then he lets them go again. He *lives* off burgers and chips, hence his waistline."

"That's not true. I give them to my Missus, she prefers her food fresh. But I've already told you that!".

"So you get High Maintenance Mindy to do the honours, do you? Lazy, that's what you are!"

Lady Serena saw that they were showing off again and told them to be quiet. "If you are going to play well together, you need to gather a sense of camaraderie. Team spirit. Like the Beatles."

"The who?" screeched Screecher.

"No. You heard her... she said the Beatles!" Gobbler rolled his eyes. "Surely even you have heard of them."

"What do you mean, even you? You are so rude to me, I'm of the mind to pack this in. It's not like I haven't got better things to do with my time."

"Like what?" Gobbler sounded genuinely interested.

Screecher found himself lost for words, which didn't happen often.

Lady Serena raised a wing. She saw Gavin approaching, all wiped clean. "That is enough. You Jingle Gulls need to start showing one another some R.E.S.P.E.C.T."

All fell silent.

None of them could spell.

It weighed heavily on Gavin's mind that time was ticking by quickly. The Jingle Gulls squabbled and fought over absolutely everything. He felt at a complete loss when it came to controlling them. Even his sergeant major style didn't seem to work. Neither did pleading or bribing.

He hadn't heard from Lady Serena, and despite her assurances that she would consult with the Seagull Songstress's manager, he felt more and more worried that they wouldn't hear from her again.

Dropper waddled into the Seaweed Café, looking very dejected. "What's the matter now?"

Dropper could barely raise his beak. "You say that like there is always something the matter with me."

"Well..." Gavin started, but thought better of it. "Anyway, I managed to find a set of drums. You did say you'd played them in the past?"

Dropper nodded, but without enthusiasm. "What's the point? I'll only keep dropping the sticks, like last time."

Stasher came dashing in just at that moment. "Am I late?"

Gavin sighed. "You are always late, but never mind. I got a set of drums for Dropper here, but he's worried he'll keep dropping the sticks."

Stasher looked thoughtful. "I've got an easy solution for that." He disappeared into the kitchen of the Seaweed Café and returned with a pot of glue. "We'll stick them to your wings and then take them off after we've finished playing. Then you can't drop them, can you?"

Dropper raised his beak, looking a little happier. "And I'm starving. Gobbler gobbled my lunch again."

Gavin tossed him a slice of pizza he'd picked up in the marketplace earlier. The things he sacrificed for the Jingle Gulls.

"Are we all here now? Can we get on and practice?"

Slowfly raised a wing. Gobbler raised his wing, Stasher raised his wing, Dropper raised his wing, and he promptly dropped the slice of pizza.

Thankfully, Gobbler managed to restrain himself.

So, now we have drums, we can play even more types of Christmas songs.

"Like what?" Slowfly wanted to know.

"Like, All I Want for Christmas is You. It's a good, upbeat one, sure to get the crowds going."

"Can we do that one where they go Eeeet's Chreeeeestmas! I could sing on that?" Screecher never gave up on his dream of singing.

"No." Gavin had no intention of letting Screecher anywhere near a microphone. Not that he needed one. "You will make everyone's ears bleed."

"I'm going to sing it anyway." Grumbled Screecher.

"So have you heard from Lady Serena?" Dropper asked, his beak dropping pizza crumbs as he spoke.

As if by magic, Lady Serena appeared behind Gavin at that very moment.

Her low, silky voice made the feathers stand up on the back of his neck.

"Good evening, Gentle Gulls."

She made them sound far more civilised than they actually were.

"I have a surprise for you."

"What what?" Screeched Screecher, clapping his wings, he loved surprises.

The gulls all stood to attention in anticipation.

Lady Serena elegantly raised her wing to make a beckoning motion towards the door of the café.

All beady gull eyes switched immediately towards the door. They gasped as three of the most stunning lady gulls they'd ever seen paraded in, as if they were on a catwalk.

"Well, shiver my timbers!" As Stasher wrapped his wings around himself in an excited self-hug, a baby duckling dropped out and hurriedly waddled away.

Slowfly gasped. "The Seagull Songstresses!" He thought he might faint. He'd only been watching them on TV through a human's house window the other week.

"This is epic!"

Lady Serena turned to address the Jingle Gulls. "Jingle Gulls, I expect you to raise your game, now that my Songstresses are here to accompany you. This will only work if you are respectful and listen to my instructions. Our manager gave the OK to this, so long as we come up with the perfect performance. If that happens, Sonica, our manager, will book us into the recording studio. We might even manage a Christmas No. 1. This is provided we sing a song written by our lyricist."

Dropper frowned. "What's a lyricist?"

"A songwriter."

The Jingle Gulls all started squawking in excitement. Lady Serena shot them a stern stare. "There will be silence whenever we are not singing." She raised a sheet of paper. "I have the song here with me. Study it, learn the words, and learn the rhythm by tomorrow. We have no time to waste."

Then she turned to the three Songstresses. "Let me introduce you to Skye." Skye wore a star pendant.

The first of the Songstresses stepped forward and bowed her head. Her piercing blue eyes glanced around the room as if trying to take them all in.

"Storm."

Storm's elegant neck also bowed forward. Her bright yellow feet moved as if she were a ballet dancer. She wore a lightning pendant.

"Soleil."

Soleil stepped forward, holding her head up high. Her eyes sparkled, and her wings gave a little flutter. She wore a sun-shaped pendant.

"Do you reckon they're their real names?" Muttered Stasher behind his wing to Gobbler. "I bet they are stage names. We should get stage names too."

"Strictly NO MUTTERING BEHIND WINGS!"

If they thought Gavin sounded like a sergeant major when he shouted, you should have seen the Jingle Gulls stand to attention when Lady Serena screeched at them.

All froze rigid and lowered their beaks.

Gavin, Gobbler, Stasher, and Screecher stood in line along the sea wall, trying to hang onto the song sheets they'd been given. They'd flown out to the coast to avoid the distractions of city life.

"Where's Dropper and Slowfly?" Gobbler wanted to know.

"I think they're still in the city. It's Friday night, and they reckon that while you're not around, they've got a good chance of grabbing some grub."

Gobbler sighed. "So when are they going to learn this song then? It's no good if only half of us know it."

"They plan to come later, once they've had a good feed-up."

Stasher stared out at the ocean. "Well, I, for one, wouldn't want to face Lady Serena and the Songstresses without knowing the words. I'm going to stay here all night if that's what it takes."

"Me too." The other two seagulls squawked in unison.

Gavin felt a strange emotion. He wasn't quite sure what it was, but it turned out to be a fleeting sense of pride in his Jingle Gulls. Hopefully Dropper and Slowfly would be quickly satisfied and fly over to join them.

"OK, let's go through it line by line.
The song is called Screech it Loud."

As the snow came down and the wind blew it around,
There came from the skies a beautiful sound.

Santa's seagulls, by the light of the moon,
could be heard singing a happy tune.
Their joyful melody filled the air,
bringing a sense of warmth and cheer.
The harmony echoed through the wintry night.
Spreading the festive spirit far and wide.

Who needs a reindeer to bring you lots of gifts
and shiny things when you've got wings?
Their feathers glisten in the silver moonlight as they swoop and glide.
Santa's Seagulls bring joy and laughter everywhere.
They fly up high, as high as the stars,
Then swoop down low to deliver.

Screech it out for all the world to hear,
The Jingle Gulls fly around with all good cheer.
Santa's Gulls are here to sing, as they spread joy and love for all to see.
With each note they sing, hearts are filled with delight.
The Jingle Gulls bring magic to the silent night.

Chorus

Screech it high, screech it low,
move your hips to the rhythm
Jingle Gulls, Santa's pals
They are here to deliver.

Rap

Hide the mince pies, put out the fries,
Leave a slice of pizza on the side.
A burger or two, we will love you,
and don't skimp on the ketchup!
We'll make sure Santa's belly is full,
with a feast that's oh so grand.
And when we're done, we'll take to the sky,
spreading good cheer across the land.

Stasher felt water in his eyes that wasn't sea spray. "Oh, that's beautiful
that is."

"Yeah, I like the rap bit at the end, can I do that bit?" Gobbler nudged
Gavin's shoulder.

Screecher screeched, "If the cap fits!"

"What is that supposed to mean?" Gobbler glared at him.

"Just sayin', trust you to want to do the only bit about food."

Gavin sighed. "C'mon, gulls, let's get on and sing it. If we sing it over and over again, hopefully the words will get stuck in our heads. Practice makes perfect."

"I'm not sure about that," said Stasher. "I've spent years practicing stashing things under my wing, but they always fall out at the wrong time."

"Tell me about it!" Sighed Gavin. "Now come on, one, two, three."

"But we don't know the melody." Screecher pointed out.

"Then we will make it up as we go along to learn the words. Lady Serena will teach us the melody when we know the words. We can chant it until then."

Before they could get beyond the second line, Dropper and Slowfly glided in.

"Sorry, we're a bit late, but y'know..." Dropper waggled his head in Slowfly's direction, and everyone nodded knowingly.

They pulled out their song sheets from beneath their wings and stared at the words.

Slowfly groaned, "I ain't never going to remember all of this!"

Gobbler glared at him. "That's a defeatist attitude when you've only just landed. We've been waiting for you for half an hour, and I've learned the rap bit already."

Slowfly stared at the rap verse. "Well, no surprises there then."

Just as Dropper held his song sheet up to study it, a gust of wind pulled it away from him. The gulls all watched the paper float away, out to sea.

"Trust Dropper." Gobbler squawked, laughing loudly.

A couple hurried past them along the promenade, clutching paper wrappers full of fish and chips. Gobbler's neck snapped around to watch them.

No!" Gavin let out a panicked shriek. "For once in your life, Gobbler, forget food and concentrate on this!"

"Keep your beak on! I am concentrating. I know the rap verse already. What have the other Jingle Gulls learned, eh? Eh?"

A man with a gnome-like beard approached them. "Wassup with you gulls tonight? You're all of a squitter."

The gulls ignored him; they knew better than to try to interact with humans. It usually ended with being accused of something. Luckily, he hurried away, but not without muttering that they were a haughty lot.

Gavin raised his wings.

"I think it's best if we start off by just saying the words. Let's speak the first verse altogether and then read it out loud, one by one."

Of course, they all read at different paces.

Slowfly, naturally, was slow. Dropper had to share Gobbler's song sheet and kept complaining that Gobbler didn't hold it up high enough.

Stasher seemed distracted by something down on the pebbles below.

Gavin persisted in his efforts to get them to learn the first verse. Eventually, they started to get the hang of it.

The whiteness of the six gulls could be seen from the Mayflower pub across the road. Maisie Dixon, the landlady, stared out of the window at them. She muttered under her breath. "Them gulls are up to something. I have never seen them stand there in a row like statues before."

Screecher rubbed his eyes with his wings. "I could drop off this lamppost I am so tired," he screeched across the shopping centre to Slowfly and Gobbler.

They'd flown back from the coast together at nearly 5 a.m. the following morning.

"I'm starving." Screeched back, Gobbler. "All that work and then flying here has worked me up an appetite." His laser-sharp eyes spotted a teenager biting into a bacon roll as he sloped up the street. Gobbler liked stalking teenagers. They were a bit like Dropper; they inevitably dropped something at some point. Either they'd bump into their mates and start chatting, thereby forgetting to keep an eye on their food. Or, they'd sit at the bus stop, staring at their phone, and drop the roll or whatever it was they had in their hand. Some of them popped into the supermarkets and grabbed bags of crisps or chocolate. Gobbler always hoped a skateboarder or cyclist would come along at that point and accidentally knock the bag of crisps out of their hand. Like a Red Arrow at full speed, he would swoop down and grab every last crumb, sometimes even before it hit the floor.

Slowfly had taken to following Gobbler about. He studied his habits carefully. If any gull knew where to get the best feed, it was Gobbler. Slowfly wasn't anywhere near as fast, but at least this way, he found out where the richest pickings were. He would have shared this with Dropper, but Dropper always seemed so negative about everything, so he kept quiet. Plus, there was only so much food to go around.

Meanwhile, Dropper patiently bobbed on the city river alongside the swans, wishing he could be a swan. The humans loved swans. They fed them and cooed over how pretty they were. Even being a pigeon would be better than being a seagull. Humans seemed to love pigeons for no fathomable reason he could find.

You've never heard a person exclaim, "What a beautiful seagull!" Or "Isn't that seagull cute?" Never.

Dropper figured that if he hung out with the swans and pigeons, it might be easier to get food from humans. They would throw it instead of him having to wait for them to drop it or leave it outside on a restaurant table (which rarely happened in the winter months).

Dropper's advantage over the swans was that he could move quicker than them. They would get a bit hissy and snarly at times, but it was easier than fighting aggressive seagulls. The pigeons were a bit dopey, so it was no trouble to get around them. He hung out at the back of a group of pigeons, waited for the human to spill the crumbs, seed, or whatever, then casually barged his way in, scattering the pigeons with his size. Sometimes the humans shouted at him to go away, and sometimes they took pity on him. He spent a lot of time practicing a sorrowful expression in the mirror, and he also found that adopting a little limp helped to encourage sympathy.

He'd never eat as well as Gobbler, but sometimes all you needed was to survive.

Gavin couldn't quite believe it. A miracle occurred. All the Jingle Gulls turned up bang on time for their rehearsal with Lady Serena and the Seagull Songsters at the Seaweed Café.

"I'm going to have to sit down for a minute." He batted his forehead with a wing, as if about to faint.

Stasher stared at him for a moment, then dashed to the counter, returning with a jug of water, which he promptly poured over Gavin's head.

"What the...!" Gavin shot up, violently shaking his feathers. "What was that for?" He turned on Stasher, his eyes blinking with confusion.

"I thought you were fainting."

Were these gulls ever going to grow up? Gavin wiped himself off with a tea towel.

This time, it was Lady Serena who arrived late.

The Jingle Gulls grumbled for the full 20 minutes, that the Songstresses kept them waiting.

Gavin smirked to himself. At last, they knew how he felt when they kept him waiting.

Eventually the door flung open and Lady Serena glided in, the Songstresses fluttering along in her wake. The Jingle Gulls immediately stopped chattering and stood to attention.

"The north wind is blowing in the wrong direction." Was all Lady Serena gave by way of apology, which was no apology at all.

She eyed the Jingle gulls. They were a motley crew. The one on the end looked shifty; there was some kind of bulk under his wing. The one next to him seemed a forlorn little fellow with pleading eyes. In the centre of the cafe, the one known as 'Gobbler' had a puffy chest, and his beak seemed brighter than the others. Next to him stood the one with the wonky beak and the handsome one, Gavin. The last one stood statue still, staring hard at the songstresses as if waiting for a cue to breathe.

Still, maybe the general public would take to their quirky characters. You could never predict.

"So, have you learned your lines?"

Gavin stepped forward, his bright yellow feet glowing in the café lamplight, his beak up high. "I am very happy to say we have!" Under his breath, he whispered to her, "You look beautiful tonight."

Gobbler also stepped forward. "We didn't know the tune, so we spoke it until we knew every line." He puffed out his chest. "I'm very good at the rap bit. Do you want to hear?"

Lady Serena waved him away with a swoop of her wing. "Not at the moment, thank you. I want you all to recite the words together, and in time."

Gavin felt a tide of nervousness wash over him. He cleared his throat. "OK, Jingle Gulls, after my count of three."

"As the snow came down..." Stasher blurted it out before Gavin could get to three.

Gavin sighed. "AFTER, the count of three."

So forceful was his screech that Stasher dropped the hamster he had under his wing, and it darted straight between Lady Serena's feet. She leapt up in alarm.

Gobbler sniggered loudly. Dropper flapped a wing in front of his face, unable to look.

Gavin pretended he hadn't seen it and carried on counting.

Then something truly remarkable happened. The Jingle Gulls all started to recite the words in unison. This went perfectly until they got to the rap bit, when Gobbler decided to show off by dancing and raising his voice above the others.

"Goodness me," screeched Screecher. "He seems to think he's auditioning for Seaweed Café's Got Talent or something. What a show-off!"

Lady Serena's eyes were glassy. "I am impressed, Gavin! You managed to pull it off. I didn't believe you would."

Gavin didn't quite know whether to take this as a compliment or not.

"So now we can get to work with the music." She indicated that Storm should hand out the music sheets.

The Jingle Gull's hearts sank as they looked at the music sheets with their strange black strokes and dots. Everything they'd learned before, they'd learned by ear. They didn't have a clue how to read musical notes.

"Oh, er, gosh, is that the time? I promised Mrs Slowfly we could go for fish and chips tonight." Slowfly started to back towards the door.

"Oh no, you don't!" Gavin raced around behind him, snapping at his rear to stop him from escaping through the door.

Stasher, fascinated, stared hard at the music sheet. "Is it some kind of code?"

"You could say that." Was there anything they could do with ease? Lady Serena raised her wings towards the Songstresses. "Let the Songstresses sing it to you, then maybe you will pick up on the melody from them." Despite her misgivings, her tone was kind.

The Songstresses stepped forward daintily, as if they were ballet dancers.

Dropper's beak dropped open in awe.

There was no visible count, but Gavin noticed Lady Serena subtly twitch her wing. All the Songstress's eyes were upon it.

The Jingle Gulls, up on the flat roof, stared at the view across to the cathedral. They were uncharacteristically silent.

Eventually, Gobbler spoke, emphasising each and every word. "That had to be the most amazing sound I have ever heard. In all of my life."

The Jingle Gulls all nodded, their eyes brimming with tears at the recollection of the Songstress's singing their Christmas song.

Eventually Slowfly spoke, his voice quiet, as if defeated. "Maybe we should just let them get on with it. We will never be as good as they are."

This snapped Gavin out of his trance. "No way! We are the Jingle Gulls, and we are just as good as them. A little rougher around the edges...

"A little?" Snorted Stasher.

"Look, you lot are always griping about not getting enough food, not flying off on holiday, not getting the kindest gull friends. Do this well, and you will get anything you want! We will be famous. Also, we will be able to make a large donation to the charity we are doing it for. We will be heroes!" Gavin raised himself to his full height, his beak in the air.

"Yeah, just for one day. Then everyone will forget about us." Dropper hung his head.

Gobbler groaned. "C'mon, Dropper, who could forget us? We are unique!"

"You mean odd." Stasher fumbled with something under his wing.

Gavin glared at him. "You are the odd one! What on earth have you got under your wing now? Surely there's not a creature left we haven't seen yet. Let the poor thing go and concentrate on the job-in-wing. For goodness sake, Mindy must be a horse, never mind a seagull!"

"SHE'S NOT A HORSE!"

Gobbler squawked with laughter. "Gavin means she must have an appetite like a horse, not that she is an actual horse."

Things never changed, thought Gavin. The Jingle Gulls were impossible to pull together as a band. Perhaps he could join the Songstresses on his own and let this unruly lot get back to their lives swooping around, causing mayhem.

"Did you notice how the Songstresses took Lady Serena's cue—a mere twitch of her wing—and they all came in perfectly on time? Shall we try something similar?"

Dropper shook his head miserably. Gobbler looked vague. Stasher dropped a mouse out from under his wing and stared mournfully after it as it scurried off across the flat roof. He nodded, but he hadn't noticed the cue. He thought the Songstresses had to be angels, not of this world. He couldn't identify with them at all.

Screecher started screeching because he thought he saw an owl circling up above. It turned out to be a drone that a teenager was flying down on the pavement below.

"OK." Gavin groaned inwardly, but a gritty determination swept over him. If he could train the Jingle Gulls to be as good as the Songstresses, what a powerful combination it would be. He adopted his sergeant major squawk again. "I want you all to stand in line. Raise yourselves to equal heights. Puff out your chests. Wings by your sides. Yes, that includes you, Stasher. Forget looking for that mouse. It's gone."

"It's my pet."

Gobbler snorted. "Since when did gulls have pets? You really are priceless, Stasher."

"It's Mindy's pet."

"QUIET!" Gavin glared at them. "When I speak, you listen. When I screech, your legs will wobble, but your mind will focus. When I twitch my left wing, you will start singing."

Stasher, Screecher, and Dropper immediately stared at Gavin's wings, confused.

Gobbler pointed to Gavin's left wing. "That one."

Slowfly blinked, not daring to breathe.

Gavin flicked his left wing, and the Jingle Gulls broke into song.

They weren't in time. Gavin raised his wing to halt them.

For three hours, he put the Jingle Gulls through their paces until Gobbler mock-fainted.

They all gathered around Gobbler, cautiously poking at him with their webbed feet. He opened one of his beady eyes to squint at them. "Lack of sustenance. I can't work this hard without food."

"I know a good place to go." The words were out of Dropper's beak before he could think. With all eyes upon him, he had no choice but to spill the beans, or, as it turned out, the biscuit crumbs.

A new café a few streets away from the flat roof had recently opened its doors.

The gulls strategically positioned themselves on lampposts opposite.

"Taking the Biscuit Café." Gobbler read the signage out loud. "That's what you are doing Dropper, taking the biscuit. You've brought us over here to gather crumbs? That's not going to satisfy my hunger pains."

As he spoke, an elderly lady with shaky hands wobbled out of the cafe and dropped a plate of biscuits into the street.

Dropper swooped straight down, swept up a whole custard cream in his beak, and strutted over to the curb with it. He glanced up to see the other gulls all swooping down to join him. In seconds, every biscuit was gone.

"She does that every day at exactly the same time. It's a rare thing, but she seems to like us gulls."

"Very nice," spluttered Gavin, gobbling up a Garibaldi. "Thanks for sharing, Dropper. I don't want you gulls coming here every day. We don't want to get too tubby in case we end up on TV."

"You are kidding, aren't you?" Stasher stared at the heap of chocolate cookies heaped up under his wing. "Mindy will eat most of these." He added quickly.

Gobbler squawked. "I reckon Mindy is your imaginary bird friend. Any of you beady-eyed guzzlers ever seen her?

Dropper, Slowfly, and Screecher all shook their heads.

Gavin, swallowing the last crumb of a Jammy Dodger, nodded his. "I have. I met her on the pier at Cromer one day. A delightful seagull, most charming."

Stasher looked relieved.

The gulls gathered up the remaining crumbs scattered on the tarmac, screeching their thank yous to the elderly lady, they flew off back to the flat roof.

Stasher flew alongside Gavin. "Thanks Gavin. I didn't know you'd met Mindy."

"That's because I haven't. She doesn't exist does she Stasher?"

Stasher groaned. "No."

"Thought as much. Now, do me a favour, stop hiding things under your wing, and concentrate on singing. That way I will feel better able to keep your secret."

Me and my shadow, thought Gavin as he caught sight of Stasher mirroring his every move. At least he had quit stashing creatures under his wing in the pretence they were for his imaginary bird friend Mindy. What was all that about?

Gobbler couldn't get over how Stasher had changed. "Has Gavin hypnotised you?"

Stasher *ignored* him.

At rehearsals that night, Stasher hung on Gavin's every word, obeyed every instruction, and waited on his leader wing and beak.

"Slowfly, Dropper, Screecher, do you know why Stasher has suddenly turned into Gavin's mini-me?" Gobbler asked.

The three gulls were dumbfounded too. "Bizarre, ain't it?" Screecher gazed across the cafe at Stasher as he dutifully waddled around behind Gavin.

"Well," said Dropper, folding his wings defensively, "I hope it's not infectious. I don't want to end up like that too."

"This is the first time I've known him to turn up for rehearsals without some little creature under his wing. It smells fishy to me."

"Except there doesn't appear to be a fish." Gobbler replied with a hint of disappointment.

"Why don't you ask him?"

"No, you ask him, Dropper."

"Why me?"

"He likes you best."

Dropper didn't agree. "He usually flies around with Slowfly. Why can't he ask him?"

Their voices rose into a crescendo of squawks as they argued. Gavin came strutting over, Stasher close behind.

"Are you ready to start rehearsals? Lady Serena and The Songtresses will be here shortly."

"Why haven't you got anything under your wing, Stasher?" Gobbler could no longer contain himself.

Stasher immediately looked sheepish. He couldn't do right by doing wrong. "I'm not that hungry today."

"But you never eat them anyway." Pointed out Dropper.

Gavin raised a wing. "Enough! Stasher has agreed not to stash things under his wing, as he knows how badly it can disrupt rehearsals. If only you were as responsive to my requests."

He stared at them. "Now, grab your instruments and let's have a quick pre-rehearsal."

Soon the Jingle Gulls forgot all about Stasher and his odd behaviour as they threw themselves into giving the Christmas song their best. They all wanted to impress the Songstresses when they arrived.

When Lady Serena arrived, she had some important news for the Jingle Gulls. A camera crew followed her and the Songstresses into the Seaweed Café.

She raised her wings to stop their playing. "Birdtastic Productions is making a documentary about the Songstresses. It is called The Making of a Super Seagull Band."

Gavin, whose heart always pounded at the sight of Lady Serena anyway, felt even weaker at the knees than usual. For once, he found himself lost for words.

"Gavin the Gull is the leader of the Jingle Gulls. He masterminded their Christmas song Screech it Loud, and we are all singing it to raise money for a charitable cause that will help less fortunate gulls."

Lady Serena waved her wing at a familiar-looking gull holding a microphone. "Gavin, this is Glen De Havilland, the famous TV presenter from True Gull Stories."

Awestruck, Dropper's beak dropped open wide. "But that's my favourite TV programme ever!" He stuttered in awe.

"Delighted to meet you." Gavin recomposed himself and waved his wing in greeting.

Glen de Havilland pushed the microphone at Gavin's beak. "Delighted to meet you too, Gavin. I've heard a lot about your efforts with the Jingle Gulls. I hear you are whipping them into shape to form a super seagull band with Lady Serena and the Songstresses."

"Um, that's right."

Gobbler didn't like the way the presenter said 'whipped them into shape.' "We are all super talented, actually."

Slowfly and Dropper grunted in agreement.

"If it's alright with you, Gavin, I'd like to interview each of your Jingle Gulls to find out their personal stories."

Glen de Havilland had a smooth way about him that left Gavin feeling most uneasy.

He could only imagine what the Jingle Gulls would come out with. He tried to look unfazed. "Certainly, but does that have to be tonight? We are on a tight schedule and need to get on with our rehearsal."

Glen gave Lady Serena a sidelong look. "Our filming schedule is tight too. We need to get this wrapped up tonight. It will be fantastic publicity for you all. We air the programme on Monday night. Perfect timing, as I believe your song will be out the day after."

"Ah, I see."

"And of course, I will need your story first."

Gavin asked for a little alone time to talk to his Jingle Gulls.

"Now listen. Stick to the positives. No one wants to know how you are always dropping things, Dropper, or how slow you are at flying Slowfly, and they certainly don't need to hear about your gobbling antics, Gobbler, and how you are always stealing food right out under the beaks of others."

Gobbler narrowed his beady eyes. "What about Stasher? Won't they want to know about his habit of storing live, defenceless little creatures under his wing?"

Gavin and Stasher glared at him.

"I HAVEN'T GOT ANYTHING UNDER MY WING!" Stasher squawked, outraged at the suggestion, even though this was the first night ever, that he didn't have a creature stashed under his wing.

Screecher screeched with laughter.

"Like I said, be positive. Say only nice things, and you can't go wrong." Gavin puffed his chest out. "And that's an order. We can't afford to mess this up."

The Jingle Gulls shuffled back to where the film crew was. Gavin told Glen they were ready to be interviewed.

"You first." The TV presenter indicated for a light to be shone on Gavin, and a microphone was swiftly clipped to a feather on his neck.

Glen de Havilland, the world-famous gull presenter, smiled charmingly at him.
"So, here we are with the Jingle Gulls. How did you all meet?"

Gavin felt his throat go dry. He didn't want to say they'd met at a rubbish tip during the 2020 pandemic, when food was scarce and all the humans were locked away. It didn't exactly screech glamour or romance. He glanced over at Lady Serena. She didn't know the truth either. His hesitancy prompted Stasher to answer, who was, of course, standing as close as he possibly could to Gavin.

"We met at a rubbish dump," he squawked. "Filthy wretch of a place, but we couldn't find food anywhere else, on account of the pandemic."

Gavin groaned; he couldn't bring himself to look at Lady Serena. If he had, he'd have seen a knowing, sympathetic look in her eye.

"Times were the hardest in living memory for us gulls. Instead of fighting over food, we bonded and helped one another. That's why we are singing this song, it's to help gulls that landed up in a similar position to us and who continue to have problems thanks to global warming, the sewage in rivers, and all the garbage that gets dumped at sea."

A spontaneous clapping of wings erupted around the cafe. Gavin dared to glance at Lady Serena and saw her wipe away a tear.

"That's such a moving story," Glen de Havilland sounded a little choked himself. He turned to Stasher. "And you, Stasher, I'm guessing you have that name for a reason?"

Stasher looked uncomfortable, but encouraged by the sympathetic atmosphere that now permeated through the cafe, he stared into the camera. "Not having enough food at that time had a big effect on me. You never know when another pandemic or some such disaster might strike, so I started stashing things away. Well, to be honest, small creatures I never eat because I don't have the heart to. I always end up letting them escape. Everyone laughed at me, so I made up a bird friend who came to be known as High Maintenance Mindy and said they were for her."

Stasher heard Gobbler sniggering in the background and stared straight at him. "The thing is, some gulls don't have any sense of camaraderie and will snatch food right out from under your beak. So, you have to be careful."

Dropper stepped forward. "Yeah, I can vouch for that. I was born with weakness in my wings, so I have a habit of dropping food. Some gulls just grab it before I get a chance to pick it up again. There have been times when I nearly starved because of it. The truth is, I hang out with swans and pigeons these days because they get fed by humans. It's easier.

Glen de Havilland stared at Dropper for a moment, then turned to the camera himself. "There you have it—hard times indeed for seagulls. The Jingle Gulls are doing a magnificent job here in raising awareness."

Turning back, he gestured to Slowfly, who shyly came forward.

"Tell me, you with the bent beak, what's your story?"

"I DON'T HAVE A BENT BEAK!" Screeched Slowfly. He hated it when anyone pointed it out. Especially as it was obviously bent.

"OK, a differently shaped beak." Glen smoothly placated him.

Gobbler stepped in. "It is tough on Slowfly, as whether he likes it or not, his beak is bent—er, I mean, how did you put it, differently shaped?" He placed a protective wing across Slowfly's back. "The thing is, he's the kindest gull you could ever wish to meet. He's super patient and will give you his last herring, however hungry he is. However, his aerodynamics, caused by his... um, differently shaped beak, slow him down considerably. We try to create our own airstreams to help him along by forming a special flight formation around him."

Slowfly nodded. "The Jingle Gulls have saved my life on many occasions, simply by being the wind beneath my wings. It's all very well for humans to think we should just fly out to sea and go fishing. When our wings are feeling weak or our beak isn't aerodynamic enough, this can be an impossibility."

Glen seemed impressed. "And you, Gobbler, it seems you don't have the best reputation?"

Typical journalist, thought Gobbler, going for the jugular. "Why am I called Gobbler?" He stared into the famous TV presenter's eyes. "That's an easy one to answer. When food was scarce, I gobbled down anything I could, desperate to survive, and sadly, it became a habit. I have it in my head that food supplies could dry up at any time. I had to watch my parents fade away through starvation, and I don't want to go the same way. I'm not proud of my name, but it's gobbling that keeps me alive."

The TV presenter looked duly chastened. He quickly turned away towards Screecher. "Screecher, are you the singer in the band?"

Talk about hitting a sore spot, thought Gavin.

Screecher shook his head. "No, not everyone likes my voice. Apparently, it's too loud. The reason I screech is because I got trapped in the rubbish dump while trying to pull a chicken carcass from under a vacuum cleaner. The only thing that saved me was my screeching. Gavin heard me and, along with the other gulls, managed to pull me free. They saved my life. If it wasn't for them, I'd have perished beneath that Hoover."

Glen de Havilland indicated for the camera gull to pan around the room. "So there we have it. A brave flock of gulls who have been there for one another at the hardest of times. I would urge you to rush out and buy their Christmas song the moment it is released on Wednesday. All funds go to helping gulls in trouble, which could, and often has been, each and every one of us."

Lady Serena took a deep breath. "Oh my goodness, what a powerful programme you have to air, Glen! I feel quite overcome with emotion."

Gavin stepped forward to offer her a warm-winged embrace, but much to his disappointment, Glen reached Lady Serena first.

"He's in a foul mood today." Dropper nodded his head to indicate Gavin's direction. "I don't know what's been ruffling his feathers, but he's snapping at everyone. I thought he'd be pleased that last night went so well."

Gobbler, his beak full, nodded in agreement.

Screecher scowled. "He nearly beaked me in the eye when I asked if we could go to the Taking the Biscuit Café again today."

Stasher hovered in the vicinity of Gavin, but even he was careful to give him some space.

Gobbler swallowed. "Maybe the pressure is getting too much for him. We're due to go to the recording studio in a couple of days to record the song, ready for release."

"Last night went really well, though. Even the songstresses seemed happy with us. Lady Serena said it was the best rehearsal ever."

"Ah, Lady Serena." Gobbler wobbled his head.
"Laydeeeee Sereeeeena..." He swivelled his eyes towards Gavin and then back again.

Dropper's beak dropped open. "What?"

Gobbler repeated the words and motion.

Screecher shrieked. "Laydeeeeee Sereeeeeeena." He mimicked Gobbler, wobbling his head and swivelling his eyes towards Gavin.

Unfortunately, Screecher's screech came out a lot louder than Gobbler's, and Gavin heard him.

Fury crossed his face, he flapped his wings, and he soared off into the sky.

Stasher, caught off guard, failed to spot him leaving. He spun around to stare at Gobbler, Screecher, and Dropper. "Where'd Gavin go?"

Gobbler raised his eyes heavenward. "Off to sulk over Lady Serena, I suspect. Screecher here, screeched a bit too loud."

"You started it." Screecher screeched.

"Not the point," retorted Gobbler, chuckling.

Gavin flew at great speed over the fields and across the streams and rivers below. Higher and higher, he flew. The wind whistled past him. He wanted to get to the sea and hear the crash of the waves. He needed noise to drown out his thoughts. He blinked his eyes, trying to shut out visions of Lady Serena. Never had there been such an intelligent, talented, and beautiful gull in his life. What would she want with a regular gull like him? He knew the answer. He'd seen the way she stretched her neck to gaze into Glen de Havilland's eyes. The handsome gull presenter with suave good looks, fame, and a never-ending supply of free fish thrown to him wherever he went.

Gavin swallowed down the bile rising in his throat.

The Jingle Gulls would never understand his pain. They were a good flock, but they lacked vision and ambition. Ever since the day he'd first launched himself off an office building into the air below as a young chick, Gavin sought to reach new heights in his life. He'd hoped forming the Jingle Gulls would launch them out of the mire of drudgery of searching for food every day. Fighting with other gulls for morsels, simply to survive.

Gavin didn't want merely to survive; he wanted to live. He wanted to achieve great things—to be the gull he always felt he could be.

In the pit of his stomach, his deep fear was that once the song had been recorded, if it flopped in the Top of the Gull Charts, the chance to launch the Jingle Gulls into a new stratosphere would be lost.

It wasn't simply about wanting to impress Lady Serena (although obviously that was a factor). It was about *lifting the self-belief* of a gang of gulls who had all been through awful times. He wanted them to believe, as he did, that they could achieve great things. Fly to new heights. Seeing the reactions of the gull film crew to their stories and of Lady Serena herself had rocked him to the core. The weight of responsibility felt crushing.

Higher and higher he *flew*, eager to reach the sea and *feel* the calming effects of the spray. The vast ocean, where their lives seemed so small and insignificant, beckoned. Nothing overwhelmed him like the sea; there, he knew his troubles would evaporate. He needed to reinvigorate, to return, head held high, ready to sing the Christmas song, and see what fate might bring next.

At last, seeing the powerful light of the lighthouse beaming out, Gavin swooped down onto the cliff edge to rest his wings. A few gulls screeched to him that a storm was coming. He didn't care.

Stasher paced up and down the flat roof, miserable and alone. Where had Gavin gone? He'd stopped stashing things under his wing at Gavin's request, and now Gavin had abandoned him. Such was his despair that Stasher didn't even feel like going to look for a comforting duckling or mouse to stash under his wing, in revenge for being left all alone.

Slowfly glided down beside him. "What's up with you?"

"Gavin's gone." Stasher squawked miserably.

"But he'll be back. Don't worry." Slowfly didn't like seeing his friend so sad.

"How do you know? He's lovesick for Lady Serena. I reckon he's flown away because he has no hope with her."

Slowfly gazed up into the hazy sky. "Whether he has hope with Lady Serena or not, he will be back. This Christmas song and looking after us gulls mean everything to him. Have faith, my friend, Gavin will be back."

But as the hours passed, even Slowfly began to feel concerned that Gavin might not come back. No one knew what any gull might do if spurned in love, or anything else for that matter.

They were all such tempestuous creatures.

Gobbler, Dropper, and Screecher swooped in. Dropper dropped a lump of burger as he landed, and Gobbler, without a second thought, gobbled it up immediately.

Dropper sighed but said nothing.

"Oops, sorry, force of habit."

Gobbler didn't look particularly sorry, but seeing Stasher's teary eyes, Dropper decided to drop the subject, just as he'd dropped the burger.

"No sign of Gavin then?" Screecher screeched. Tact had never been his thing, not that any gull had any great habit of tact.

Stasher gazed longingly up at the sky.

Gobbler clapped his wings. "While we're waiting for our illustrious leader to return, may I make a suggestion?"

Dropper stared at him. "What?"

Gobbler pointed a wing at the position of the sun. This is how seagulls tell the time. "It's biscuit time. I vote we wing off to the Taking the Biscuit Café for a spot of sustenance."

"But Gavin said..."

"Well, we don't have to always tell Gavin everything, do we? A few biscuits will cheer us all up, and like you said, it's not often a human cares to feed us without a little, er, shall we say, prompting?"

"Oh, very well then." Stasher felt so low, he couldn't be bothered to put up any resistance to the idea.

Delighted, Dropper flapped up into the sky, waiting for Slowfly to join him.

The five gulls flew off to the Taking the Biscuit Café, Slowfly safely in the middle so he could be swept along.

Gobbler, as ever, the first gull to land, gazed longingly at the door of the cafe, waiting for the elderly lady to appear. The other gull's feet slapped down on the pavement beside him.

"So what's your favourite biscuit, Stasher?" Gobbler intended to grab Stasher's favourite to give to him in an attempt to cheer him up.

Stasher stared at the sky. "Dunno."

"I like those soft ones with dark paste in." Slowfly found them easier on his beak.

"Fig rolls." Confirmed Screecher. "That's what they are."

Dropper fancied one with icing. "I like sugary stuff. I know it's bad for me, but we almost never eat sugar."

"After we've recorded the song, I reckon we should all treat ourselves to a proper fishing trip at the coast. Mackerel is my dream fish. I can't get enough of it. That way, we will all be fit when we do more TV appearances. We need to look good next to the Songstresses."

Gobbler wanted to sound as positive as Gavin usually did. If, by some terrible chance, Gavin didn't come back, he needed to prepare himself to take over as leader. Of course, he couldn't say this out loud.

The Jingle Gulls waited patiently for the cafe door to open. Dropper wandered up the street a bit. Stasher continued to gaze at the sky. Screecher flew up to a lamppost to see if he could get a better view through the café window.

None of them liked waiting, but quite often they had no choice. Then suddenly Dropper came rushing back down the street, excitedly flapping his wings. "Quick quick! We all need to hide behind that wall!"

"Whaddya mean?" Screeched Screecher.

"Sssshh, quick behind the wall!" Dropper gestured to Screecher to get down off the lamp post to join them.

Having safely ushered them all behind the wall, Dropper poked his beak out around the corner, then jolted back again. "Lady Serena is approaching the cafe, and guess who is with her?"

"Gavin!" Squawked Stasher excitedly.

"No, it's the TV presenter, Glen de Havviwotsit."

"Stop messing about. That's not funny!" Stasher tried to look over the wall.

"Get down or they'll see you!" Dropper slapped Stasher's head down with his wing.

Gobbler tiptoed to the other end of the wall to look out. "Oh dear, you're not wrong. And they are wing in wing."

Stasher screeched in fury.

"Just kidding." Guffawed Gobbler.

"Don't be so gullible, Stasher." Dropper couldn't believe the stuff Stasher fell for sometimes.

"Of course I'm gullible. I'm a gull, for goodness sake!"

"What are they doing?"

Dropper poked his head around the wall again. "They're standing on one of the tables outside. The lady is coming out with a tray of biscuits. She's put it down next to them, but they are ignoring it."

"Too busy gazing into one another's eyes, I suppose." Stasher sighed. He really felt for Gavin.

"If only we could get closer to hear what they are saying," Slowfly gave a little jump to see what he could see.

"Get down!" Dropper glared at him.

Gobbler couldn't bear it. The thought of the untouched tray of biscuits was driving him crazy. Suddenly, he launched himself high up into the air and swooped down towards the tray, grabbing a biscuit in his beak. Before either Lady Serena or Glen de Havilland could look up, he had gone.

Moments later, Gobbler swooped in again, but this time he lost his balance on the table and tipped the whole tray onto the floor. Lady Serena recognised him right away. "Gobbler! Is that you?"

Gobbler turned to her, his beak full and his eyes wide. Glen de Havilland, annoyed, screeched at Gobbler. "Watch what you are doing! You nearly toppled Lady Serena off the table."

Gobbler would have apologised, but he was too busy munching a digestive.

Watching the whole scene from around the side of the wall, Dropper, Screecher, and Slowfly decided that now that their cover had been blown, they may as well join Gobbler in devouring the biscuits. They all flew over and began grabbing biscuits without so much as a hello.

"Where are your manners?"

"Oh, let them eat! They are starving the poor things."

Lady Serena couldn't believe that Glen had already forgotten their sorry tales from the previous night.

"Where's their leader?"

"He's gone!" Blurted out Stasher before anyone could stop him.

Lady Serena frowned. "What do you mean, gone?"

"He's gone, and we don't know if he's coming back." Stasher felt his eyes welling up.

"But why? Why would he go? We have the recording session tomorrow. I know he was excited about it because he told me." Lady Serena began to get in a bit of a flap.

The gulls were shocked. They thought Lady Serena was an ice queen. She'd been unflappable through every situation so far.

"We'll go and look for him." Slowfly wanted to calm things down. He suddenly felt a strong sense of panic that Gavin wouldn't come back. He'd not been too worried until he saw Lady Serena's reaction to the news.

Energised by all the biscuits he had gobbled, Gobbler agreed. "Yes, let us think about where he might be."

The Jingle Gulls gathered together on the flat roof. "Slowfly, you stay here in case he comes back. Blabber is over on the flat roof opposite. If Gavin returns while we are gone, send Blabber to find us. We will do a sweep of the city, then the outlying villages. If it comes to it, we'll head to the coast."

Slowfly nodded. He knew he had to stay because they needed to fly fast, and he'd never be able to keep up.

He watched as his gull friends lifted off into the cloudy sky. He hoped they would find Gavin quickly; he didn't like being on his own.

Gobbler led the Jingle Gulls out over the rooftops; they flew in formation with him at the front, Stasher to his left wing, Screecher to his right, and Dropper bringing up the rear. They swooped into a shopping centre and asked a few gulls if they'd seen Gavin, but they hadn't.

They circled the cathedral, then dropped onto the castle roof for a few moments, but saw no sign.

The Jingle gulls flew straight down the River Wensum through the city, keeping an eye on lampposts and bridges, take-aways, and rubbish bins, hoping to catch sight of Gavin. But he wasn't anywhere to be seen.

"OK," screeched Gobbler, "let's try some of the villages we've been to before, and then head to the coast. I have a hunch that's where he will be."

For once, no gull argued.

As the sun rose, the Jingle gulls arrived back on the flat roof. They looked in a sorry state after flying around all night.

Stasher slumped down, his eyes half-closed, utterly defeated. "No idea," he muttered. "We don't know where he is."

Slowfly, the freshest of them all, flew off for another look around the city. "He has to be somewhere. Gulls simply don't disappear."

Stasher wasn't so sure; anything could have happened.

Dropper stared at Gobbler, who'd found himself a piece of pizza on the way back and was now devouring it. "How can you eat at a time like this?"

Gobbler glanced up, confused. "I can eat at any time. It doesn't mean I don't care. My belly doesn't know Gavin's missing."

"So what are we going to do about the recording later? We can't do it without Gavin."

Gobbler tossed the last bit of his pizza over to Stasher, who didn't see because he had his eyes shut.

"We will turn up and do it. It won't be the same without Gavin, but this is our big chance. We shouldn't give up. Besides, it's not just us, Lady Serena and the Songstresses have worked hard on it too."

"I don't want to." Stasher mumbled.

"Wherever Gavin is, whatever he is doing, he will want us to do this. Besides, it's not just about us. What about the gulls we are trying to help?"

"They can help themselves," said Screecher, "we had to."

A voice from behind made him jump out of his skin. "So, despite all you said in your interview, you don't care as much as you claimed?"

Screecher spun around to find Glen de Havilland standing right behind him.

"He does, he does!" Gobbler squawked defensively. "We are all worn out from flying around trying to find Gavin. It er... it came out wrong."

"Hmm, no luck then?" Glen narrowed his eyes. "Maybe you gulls should leave it to Lady Serena and the Songstresses. After all, they are professionals. Any money raised will still go to the gulls in need."

"No chance!" Dropper stretched his neck up to equal Glen de Havilland's height. "We are the Jingle Gulls, and we are very talented, I'll have you know. We've spent hours perfecting the song, and we are equal to the songstresses."

Glen snorted. "Hmm, well, let's see if this Gavin character turns up. If not, we will have to reconsider."

Gobbler, Dropper, Screecher, and Stasher couldn't understand how someone who came across on TV as so smooth and pleasant could be such a nasty gull in real life.

Stasher stared up longingly into the sky, wishing Gavin would appear. Instead, he spotted Slowfly circling, ready to land.

"Still no sight of him." He gasped slowly as he touched down.

Stasher raised his wings over his head.

"Don't cry. That's what babies do."

"I'M NOT A BABY!" Screeched Stasher. "It's just SO sad. Gavin is in love with Lady Serena, and he thinks she's too good for him, and she's with that ghastly Glen gull, and IT'S NOT FAIR!"

Gobbler shrugged. "Life isn't fair, that's why we all ended up together. It's no good going off and sulking just because Lady Muck has got better fish to fry."

"No one is better than Gavin!" Stasher flew at Gobbler, his eyes blazing with anger and his sharp beak ready to attack.

"ENOUGH!" Screeched Screecher spread his wings to keep them apart.

A terrible shriek came from above. The Jingle Gulls looked up to see the notorious Gull Gang, The Beaky Blinders, so known for the way they attacked other gulls eyes.

"Yikes! Let's get out of here." Screeched Screecher, trembling with fear.

But it was too late; the leader of the gang rocketed down beside Gobbler, making him jump out of his skin. "Your mate, Gavin, he's caught up in a storm. It's a nasty one. One of my gulls saw him clinging onto the edge of a cliff, looking in a sorry state. I apologise for bringing you bad news."

Stasher put his wings over his eyes and started to wail like a banshee.

"Thanks for letting us know."

"No bother. Some of the gang members are trying to pull him off there as we speak. He may have to rest out at the coast for a day or so if they manage to rescue him."

Dropper groaned loudly. "He won't be back for the recording."

"Gripper, we truly appreciate your gang's help with Gavin." Gobbler squawked quickly, not wanting him to hear about the recording in case he wanted in on it. The Beaky Blinders never helped anyone without some kind of payback. He'd come across them a few times. They were vicious if crossed, but they had their good points too. "We will find a way to reward their efforts, either way."

"How are we going to do that?" wailed Stasher from beneath his wing as Gripper flew off.

Gobbler glared at him. "There is always a way to reward good deeds, Stasher. Come now, stop your wailing. We will go to the recording studio and do our best without Gavin. Think how proud he will be to think that we were able to carry on. He'd hate it if we gave up."

Stasher sniffed but nodded his head in agreement.

"Let's do one last rehearsal up here before we go to the studio. We don't need the instruments. Let's sing loud and proud for Gavin."

Dropper, Screecher, and Slowfly nodded vigorously.

Stasher hung his head. "He was so kind to me, he kept my secrets and everything."

"What secrets?" Gobbler immediately wanted to know.

"THEY WERE SECRETS!" wailed Stasher. "Like I'm going to tell you."

Gobbler rolled his eyes. "Pull yourself together and shake those feathers down. Take a deep breath, and let's sing. It will make you feel better."

At first, they sounded a little weak, but by the chorus, the Jingle Gulls were in strong voice.

"Will you pesky gulls be quiet? My baby can't sleep because of you." A woman's voice yelled from somewhere down below.

The Jingle Gulls ignored her.

Gobbler decided it would be best not to tell Lady Serena and the Songstresses the real reason for Gavin's disappearance. But first, they had to deal with Glen de Havilland.

To their surprise, Glen expressed his deepest sympathies. "I am so sorry to hear your news. If there's anything at all I can do, just squawk."

"Best not mention it to Lady Serena, we don't want to put a damper on the recording."

Glen de Havilland threw Gobbler a sly look. "So what shall I tell her?"

"Bird flu."

The Jingle Gulls felt quite daunted when they saw the studio. Their eyes nearly popped out when they saw all the keyboards, buttons, and knobs.

A swaggering gull wearing sunglasses and a big gold chain showed them in. "Wassup Gulls?"

None of them had seen a seagull wearing sunglasses before, let alone a big gold chain.

"Do you think he's really a magpie?" whispered Stasher, all agog.

"It's like climbing on board a space ship," gasped Dropper as he twiddled a knob to see what would happen.

"Don't touch that!" Yelled the seagull in the sunglasses and chain, whom they later learned was known as GG the Master Mixer.

Screecher screeched into a microphone, deafening them all.

GG, the Master Mixer, grabbed it away from him. "With a gob like yours, you don't need a microphone!"

With an hour and a half to go before recording began, the Jingle Gulls were offered anchovies and cups full of sparkling, crystal-clear water to drink from. Dropper stared into his cup with suspicion. Being used to rivers or water butt water, he'd never seen anything so clear before. "Is this some kind of magic potion?"

"We look after our artists here at Seagullz Studios. Only the best." GG beckoned to his assistant, a teenage gull with a sulky look wearing a sleeveless leather tunic and an oversized baseball cap. "Bring the Jingle Gulls more anchovies, and if there's any of that nice mackerel left, lay some of that out for them too."

"I could get used to this!" Gobbler swivelled around in a large black gamer's-style chair. "It's like we are already superstars."

"Don't get too comfortable." Glen de Havilland appeared out of nowhere. "Lady Serena isn't happy at all about the no-show from Gavin. I had to persuade her to go ahead with the recording."

"Where is she?" Stasher wanted to know.

"In feathers and make-up, along with the Songstresses, they have their pre-recording routines."

"But no one will see them apart from us."

Glen rolled his eyes. "My film crew is continuing to film the story of the making of this track. You are getting star-style publicity courtesy of teaming up with Lady Serena and the Songstresses. That's why Lady Serena had second thoughts when Gavin, er, called in sick, so to speak. He's the handsome one out of this motley crew. She reckons his not being here will damage the chances of getting to No. 1."

The Jingle Gulls didn't like hearing this. They all jumped up at once and started screeching at Glen.

"Calm down. Facts are facts." GG spread his wings to push the gulls back from Glen.

"You are so rude to us!" Screecher screamed, his face red with anger. "We are all handsome gulls."

"Yes, in our own way." Agreed Gobbler. "Just because Slowfly has a bent beak, you don't have to be rude to him."

"I HAVEN'T GOT A BENT BEAK." Shrieked Slowfly.

If only Gavin was here, he'd speak up for us, thought Stasher mournfully.

Lady Serena and the Songstresses sashayed in, all pristine.

The Jingle Gulls stared down at their own dishevelled feathers.

"Now it's your turn." Lady Serena raised a wing to point towards the door.

GG's assistant sloped towards it. "This way, Jingle Gulls."

A gull with spiky head feathers and black Dr. Marten boots greeted them. "Hello, loves, let's get you looking like the pop stars you truly are. Who's going to go first?"

Gobbler looked at Dropper, Dropper looked at Screecher, Screecher looked at Slowfly, and Stasher tried to make himself invisible behind a large cardboard cutout of Simon Seagull, the famous TV talent spotter.

"Shy gulls, are we? How about you with the bent beak? I can do a bit of contouring to make it look straight."

Slowfly froze in fury but didn't say anything.

"I'm Baz, by the way. Hop up on the couch, lovey, let the transformation begin!" Baz gave Slowfly a gentle push onto the big black couch and pulled down a large ring of light from the ceiling.

"You lot, there's an anchovy vending machine over there if you are hungry."

After all the studio hospitality, even Gobbler felt full. They all sat on various stools and chairs around the make-up room, gazing in wonderment as Baz worked his magic on Slowfly.

Fifteen minutes later, Slowfly jumped off the couch, looking like a different gull. His beak appeared totally straight, and his eyes shone. His feathers were perfectly groomed, and he smelled delicious.

"To my thinking, if you feel good and look good, you can conquer the world."

"That's what we are hoping to do," agreed Gobbler, leaping forward, eager to get on the couch himself.

"I'll go next." Dropper beat him to it.

Stasher stared longingly out of the window, wondering if Gavin had been rescued yet. It felt like he was the only one who cared.

Baz added glitter to Dropper's feathers. When he finally got up off the couch, Gobbler couldn't stop laughing. "You look like a disco ball!"

Dropper did a twirl. "I'm not sure it's really me, but..."

"You look like a natural-born superstar, lovey. Own it."

Gobbler suddenly felt nervous. "Go easy on me, I've got a macho reputation to keep up." He couldn't face meeting up with the Beaky Blinders again if Baz dolled him up like Dropper.

Screecher doubled up, clutching his belly. "I think I've eaten a dodgy anchovy."

"There's a nice BMW parked outside the studio. Go do your business there." Gobbler grinned.

Screecher obediently waddled off outside.

"Nerves." Baz muttered. "Those anchovies are premium quality."

One of the Songstresses poked her head around the door. "Lady Serena wants to know *if you are nearly done*, Baz. She wants a quick vocal warm-up before the recording starts."

"Give me five." Baz waved her away. "You shouldn't hurry a genius at work. That's you done, Mr. Gobbler."

Stasher shifted uncomfortably in his seat.

"You, oh miserable-looking one. Your turn." Baz beckoned to Stasher.

"I think I look fine." Stasher didn't budge. He stared at Gobbler, whose beak shone brightly with a new diamond stud in the side of it. He saw that Gobbler's eyelashes were thicker and longer. Gobbler did look good, he had to admit, but he kept it to himself. Gobbler had a big enough ego already.

"Don't make me come over there." Baz threw him a stern look.

"OK." Stasher didn't want any trouble. Although he felt miserable without Gavin, he didn't want to let him down. He waddled over to the couch and plopped himself on it.

"I'll go find Screecher." Gobbler couldn't wait to show off his new look.

Gobbler gazed around the studio. He needed to pinch himself out of this dream. Lady Serena and the songstresses were positively glowing. He caught Soleil give him an admiring glance, and puffed his chest out.

GG The Master Mixer gathered them around for a pep talk. "First off, is every gull present and correct?"

All the gulls nodded.

Glen de Havilland signalled his camera crew of gulls to start filming. "Sadly, the Jingle Gulls aren't all quite present and correct. Gavin the Gull has been struck down with a bad case of bird flu. This is a major blow to the Jingle Gulls, as Gavin is their charismatic leader. They have bravely agreed to carry on without him for this recording."

The Jingle Gulls gathered around their instruments. Lady Serena and the songstresses moved forward, their microphones laid out in a semi-circle.

GG The Master Mixer stepped forward. "All ready?"

Gobbler checked his reflection in GG's sunglasses, and he decided he would get a pair too. That's what celebrities wore to help them get recognised in the street. Or was it to stop them from getting recognised in the street? He couldn't quite work it out. He thought that he would love to be recognised when he got famous, so he found himself in a bit of a quandary. He decided to ask GG after recording.

The camera crew moved in closer.

Slowfly whispered to Dropper, "How does my beak look?"

"Stunning." Dropper rolled his eyes.

He looked over to Stasher and Screecher. Stasher seemed to be wriggling. Dropper's heart dropped. Oh no, he thought, but it was too late to do anything about it.

The count began, and they all watched the seconds on a big digital clock with bright red numbers. When it got to 0.00, this was the cue to start playing.

Gavin's feet were sore from clinging to the rock face. Wild gusts of wind had thrown him about in the air as if he were but a single feather. Luckily, he'd been blown inland instead of further out to sea. He'd never been in such horrific conditions. The ocean roared as if furiously angry. Rain shot at him like gun pellets. Violent electric blue light shuddered down from the darkness, lighting up the sea swell. His heart beat so fast that he thought it might shatter. I never should have left the city, he thought. What a fool I am. He wondered miserably if Lady Serena would even notice his absence. He imagined the Jingle Gulls panicking without him. He'd messed up their dreams, their hopes, and their ambitions. Guilt surged through his body, and he let out a desperate cry of anger, mingled with pure misery.

Out of the darkness came a screech. "You mad gull, what are you doing there?"

Gavin thought it might be a ghost. Who else could be here? He squinted, trying to see through the driving rain.

Hovering upside down above him, he spotted a bright orange beak with scars all over it.

"Eh?"

"You stuck?"

Gavin nodded, humiliated.

"Hold on."

A high-pitched whistle pierced through the bludgeoning winds. Suddenly, through the darkness, Gavin saw several white wings flapping like crazy.

"When I say let go, Let the wind take you."

Gavin clutched even more tightly to the rock face. Letting go filled him with an extraordinary feeling—sheer terror. "I can't!"

"You will, or you will die. It is as simple as that, mate."

He looked out at the seagulls being buffeted around in the air. Who were they, and why did they want to help him?"

"Stop thinking about it and let go." The commanding shriek came from above. He did as he was told.

The air currents pushed Gavin up high. The flock of seagulls formed a protective force around him, pulling him along within their formation.

Gavin, completely exhausted, mustered just enough effort to weakly flap his wings as they carried him along in their own little airstream. "C'mon, Gavin, dig deep."

"I have to get back to the city," Gavin gasped weakly.

Soon they were free of the storm. The wind became a gentle breeze, and the sky cleared enough for shards of blue to be visible.

Gavin's wings failed him, and he began to fall to earth.

One of the gulls swooped beneath him, rose up, and carried Gavin on his back. "Don't worry, mate, we will get you home."

Gavin couldn't raise so much as a whimper; exhaustion took over, and he passed out.

When Gavin woke up, he found himself sprawled on the pavement outside of the recording studio. The gulls who'd saved him were nowhere to be seen. He wondered if he'd had some kind of fit and dreamed the whole thing.

The security guard on the door eyed him with suspicion. "Move along now. No homeless gulls are allowed here."

Gavin shook his feathers and tried to stand up, but his legs were weak and wobbly.

"I can always call the RSPB or Gull Rescue Centre if you need help." The security guard said a little more kindly. "There's no shame in asking for help, you know."

Gavin pulled himself up. "I am Gavin, from Gavin and the Jingle Gulls. We are recording our song here today with the Songstresses.

He stared down in despair at his own dishevelled feathers.

"'Course you are, mate, and I am Adam and the Ants."

"Who?"

"Let me go inside and see if some gull can vouch for you. Wait there."

The security gull took his time.

Gavin began to think he wasn't coming back. He decided to go away and get himself looking more respectable. Maybe then the security gull would believe him.

But as Gavin started to fly away, he heard a familiar screech.

58 seconds into the recording, half way through the second verse of Screech it High, with Lady Serena and the Songstresses singing happily away, swaying in unison to the music, Stasher let his wing drop, forgetting about the baby rabbit stashed away underneath it. Out it hopped. It hopped up onto Slowfly's piano, noisily jarring the keys, then it hopped onto Lady Serena's back, causing her to completely freak out.

"I'm allergic to rabbits!" She shrieked furiously. "They bring me out in hives."

"What like bee hives?" Dropper didn't understand. He gazed around the room, expecting to see bees buzzing about.

"She means red spots. I'm allergic to dumb seagulls who stash things under their wings. It gives me the same effect." Gobbler glared at Stasher.

Glen de Havilland directed one of his camera crew to catch the rabbit. "There's a box over there, stick the rabbit in that. Punch a few holes in the side so it can breathe, then make sure the lid is firmly on. We can let it go later."

GG, the Master Mixer, stared at the clock. "Let's take five. We've got the studio for another 45 minutes. That should be enough time to can it."

"Can it?" Dropper didn't get this new studio lingo.

"Back in 5, no later." GG ordered, picking up his vape.

Gobbler grabbed Stasher by the wing as he started to leave. "You pull any more stunts like that, and I will kick you out of the Jingle Gulls. Do you hear me?"

Stasher nodded. He didn't know how to explain that the rabbit had been there to comfort him. With Gavin gone, his anxiety levels were high. The cuddly little rabbit kept him calm. "Mindy wanted it." He mumbled sadly.

The seagulls all disappeared into the green room, Gobbler loudly proclaiming he'd worked up an appetite for some more anchovies.

"We hadn't even been in there a minute before you Jingle Gulls messed it up." Storm's eyes were dark and thundery.

Dropper dropped his head. "Sorry."

"We have far more to lose with our reputations than you do." Soleil added. "You are nobodies. We are famous. You better not stuff it up when we go back in there."

Screecher didn't like her tone. "You are one hit wonders. You wait and see, by this time next year, we will be more famous than you!"

Slowfly stepped in between them, spreading his wings out wide. "Let's not fight, we need to pull together."

Right there and then, Stasher decided the Jingle Gulls would be better off without him. It was he who had messed up. He edged towards the door. No gull looked his way, so he quietly opened it and tiptoed out.

What was the point anyway? Without Gavin, it all felt false and stupid. As he trundled down the corridor, he saw the security gull coming the other way. He lowered his beak, hoping the gull would pass without comment.

"Are you one of the Jingle Gulls?"

Stasher shrugged. "Er, I am... well, I was."

"There's a ragged-looking gull outside claiming to be one of your lot. Can you come out and identify him for me, so I can let him in?"

It couldn't be, could it? Stasher flew down the corridor, scattering everyone in his wake. The security guard ran after him. "Oi! Wait for me!"

Stasher dashed out of the front door, his head twisting this way and that, hoping to see Gavin. He caught sight of Gavin's tail feathers disappearing down the road. Stasher opened his beak and let out the loudest screech he'd ever projected in his entire life.

The make-up gull squinted at Gavin. "Goodness knows what I'm going to do with you in the two minutes I've been given!"

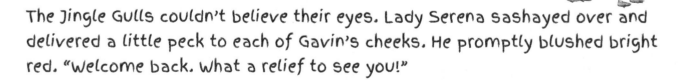

Gavin lay on the couch, looking forlorn.

"I'll help," said Stasher, his heart bursting with happiness that Gavin had arrived back safely.

Four minutes later, you would never have known what Gavin had been through, not by his appearance. His feathers were sparkling, his eyes shining, and his poor, sore feet buffeted and creamed, so they gleamed.

"By the way, you've had bird flu," whispered Stasher as they made their way to the studio.

Gavin's arrival in the studio was met with loud cheers and caws. The Jingle Gulls gathered around, delivering little pecks of happiness.

"Careful! You will undo Baz's good work."

"And mine." Stasher grinned from ear to ear.

The Jingle Gulls couldn't believe their eyes. Lady Serena sashayed over and delivered a little peck to each of Gavin's cheeks. He promptly blushed bright red. "Welcome back. What a relief to see you!"

Glen de Havilland clicked his wings, indicating to his crew that they should start filming again. "Fantastic news from the studio! The lead singer, Jingle Gull, has miraculously recovered and returned to his band. Gavin the Gull is looking better than ever and is hopefully in fine voice to get this Christmas charity song recorded. You are witnessing history in the making. This is the first Super Seagull band ever!"

GG, the Master Mixer, raised a wing. "Watch the countdown clock gulls, it's time to get this song recorded once and for all!"

The next few weeks passed in a blur. The Jingle Gulls and Lady Serena's Songstresses travelled around the country in two stretch limousines, promoting their charity Christmas single.

Every news channel and morning show wanted to interview them. It seemed like every seagull on the planet wanted their autographs. Selfies with the Super Seagull band flooded social media. Paparazzi stalked them everywhere.

"Welcome to our world." Lady Serena smiled at Gavin as they posed together with the Jingle Gulls and Songstresses on the red carpet for the latest Seagull movie, starring the world-famous superstar Steven Seagull.

In the tabloids, there were rumours of a romance between Gavin and Lady Serena, but as yet, they hadn't confirmed or denied it. She had, however, gone out of her way to make it clear that her interests in Glen de Havilland were entirely of a professional nature.

DAILY GULL

ALL THE HOT GULL GOSSIP FLOWN IN STRAIGHT TO YOU

COULD THIS BE LOVE?

GAVIN THE GULL AND LADY SERENA
INSEPERABLE AT FILM PREMIERE

Screech it Loud reached No. 1 all over the world. Sales were record-breaking.

Interviewing Gavin and Serena on his Saturday Seagull Live programme, Glen de Havilland probed as to what their relationship might be now that they were international superstars; he hoped to get a worldwide exclusive.

He plunged right in. "Never mind Jingle Bells, will we be hearing wedding bells in the near future?"

Gavin grinned, while Lady Serena kept a poker face. "We don't have a crystal ball." She reached over, placed her wing on Gavin's, and looked straight into the camera.

"But I can confirm that we are very much in love."

The live audience burst into a rapturous round of applause.

The next day, pictures of them wing-in-wing were plastered all over the tabloids, and social media positively exploded with excitement.

Gobbler, gobbling down anchovies in the green room, along with Slowfly, Stasher, Screecher, and Dropper, almost choked. "I didn't see that coming!"

They had all become so famous that the Christmas gig at the Nelson's Good Eye pub had to be moved to a nearby concert hall to cope with the huge number of seagulls who wanted to see the famous Jingle Gulls.

Millions of pounds were raised to help gulls in need. or, in their currency, fish.

Grabber gazed at his TV screen and leant back in his chair. "Well, well, well," he mewed a little sinisterly to his gang of Beaky Blinders.

"It seems we saved a superstar. We will have to think about how he will repay us..."

The story does not end here...

Find out more about Gavin the Gull by following him at
Instagram @Gavin_thegull.
Facebook/Gavin the Gull

Look out for more Gavin the Gull adventures... coming soon.

MyriadLife
Books.com